A to Z Mysteries

The Kidnapped King

by Ron Roy

illustrated by
John Steven Gurney

A STEPPING STONE BOOK™

Random House New York

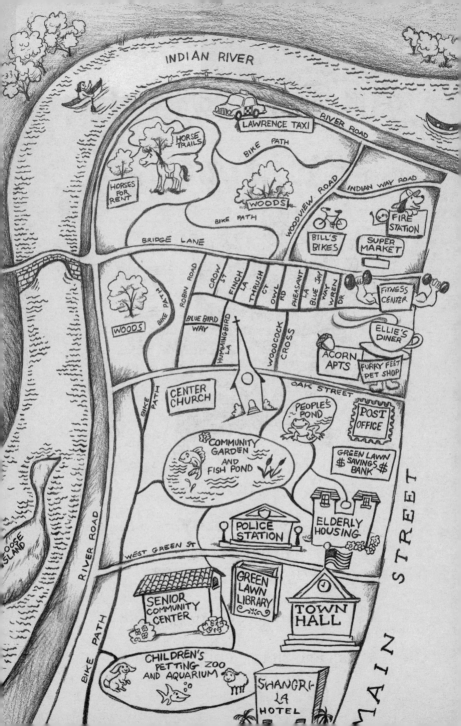

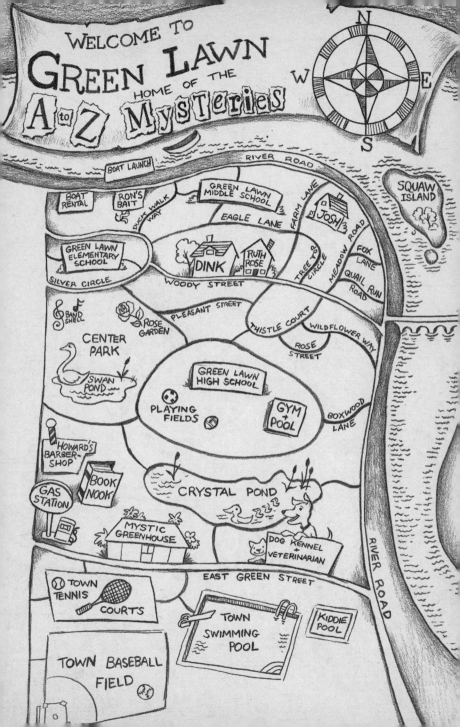

CHAPTER 1

"Done!" Dink said to himself, smiling. He had solved the last problem on his math paper. He wrote *Donald D. Duncan* at the top, then glanced up at the classroom clock: two-fifteen. In just twenty minutes, spring vacation would begin!

"Class, please get ready for DEAR time," Mrs. Eagle said. "Take out your books and find a cozy place to read until the bell rings, please."

DEAR stood for *Drop Everything and Read*. This was Dink's favorite time of the day.

Dink was reading *Kidnapped* by Robert Louis Stevenson. He had seen the movie, but he still loved the story. He took the book to the reading corner and flopped onto a beanbag chair.

Josh and Ruth Rose joined him, sprawling on the carpet with their books. The classroom grew quiet, except for the clock's ticking and the sound of pages being turned.

Suddenly, the room phone rang. Mrs. Eagle answered it, then walked to the reading corner. "Dink," she said quietly, "you're wanted in Mr. Dillon's office."

Josh grinned at Dink and raised his eyebrows. "You're in trouble!" he said.

"Mr. Dillon wants me?" Dink asked. "Why?"

Mrs. Eagle shrugged. "Hurry back," she whispered.

Dink put down his book and left the room.

Walking down the quiet hall, Dink tried to figure out why the principal wanted to see him. He couldn't think of anything he'd done wrong!

Outside Mr. Dillon's office, Dink took a deep breath, then walked in. Mrs. Waters, the principal's secretary, was sitting at her desk outside his door. She smiled. "Hi, Donald. You can go right in. And don't look so scared!" she said. "Mr. Dillon doesn't eat children!"

Dink grinned, then opened the door to Mr. Dillon's office. The first person he saw was his mother!

She patted the empty chair next to hers, and Dink slid into it.

There were three other people in the room: Mr. Dillon, a woman with

yellow hair, and a kid about Dink's age.

The kid was dressed like someone in a movie. He had on a long dark blue robe and sandals.

"Hi, Donald," Mr. Dillon said. Mr. Dillon was shaped like a football. His hair was cut short and his eyeglasses gleamed under the lights.

"Let me introduce my guests," he said. He nodded at the woman with yel-

low hair. "This is Ms. Joan Klinker. And this," he added, smiling at the boy, "is Sammi Bin Oz."

Dink mumbled, "Hi," then stared at the boy.

He was about Dink's size and had black hair and dark skin. His eyes were the color of honey.

"Sammi is from Costra," Mr. Dillon said, "a small island country in the

Indian Ocean. He's come to the United States to learn English."

"I already speak English," the boy said.

He had a soft voice and an accent. Dink thought he looked and sounded kind of sad.

"Actually, Sammi will live here for a year," Joan Klinker said. "I am his tutor. His parents want him to learn American customs."

Mr. Dillon looked at Dink. "Sammi will be in third grade with you. We thought you might want to show him around the school," he said.

Everyone looked at Dink. He felt himself blushing. His mother gave his hand a squeeze. "And Sammi will be staying with us for a few weeks, Dink," she explained.

"Your name is Dink?" Sammi asked.

Dink nodded at the boy.

"Dink," Sammi repeated. "That rhymes with *think* and *pink* and...*stink!*"

"Making rhymes helps Sammi remember new words," his tutor explained.

"Sammi can have the spare room," Dink's mother said. "With Daddy away on business, it'll be nice to have a guest in the house. I hope Sammi will be friends with you and Josh and Ruth Rose."

Sammi giggled. "*Rose* rhymes with *toes* and *nose!*"

Dink grinned. *Wait'll Josh and Ruth Rose meet* him, he thought.

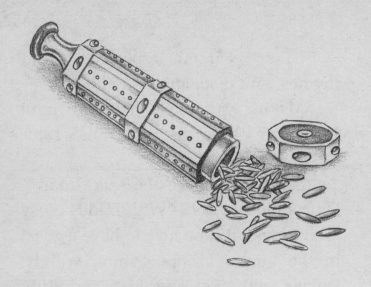

CHAPTER 2

Dink went back to class and handed a note to Mrs. Eagle. Since school was almost out, Mr. Dillon had given him permission to leave early.

Dink filled his book bag, then whispered what was going on to Josh and Ruth Rose.

Dink's mother drove him and Sammi home to Woody Street. Sammi was quiet in the car. He kept turning around and looking out the rear window.

"Ms. Klinker said she'd bring your luggage over in a little while," Dink's mother told Sammi. "Dink will help you get settled, then I'll make you both a snack."

"Thank you very much, Mrs. Duncan," Sammi said as Dink's mom pulled into the driveway on Woody Street.

Dink climbed out of the car with his book bag clunking against his shoulders.

"Your room is next to mine," he told Sammi, leading the way upstairs.

Dink took Sammi into the guest room. There was a bed, a dresser, and a braided rug on the floor. A reading lamp stood on the table next to the bed.

Sammi looked at the room quietly. "This is very nice," he said.

"Come on, I'll show you my room," Dink said. He and Sammi passed through the bathroom. On the other side was Dink's bedroom.

As soon as Dink stepped into his room, Loretta began squeaking and running around in her cage.

"What is *that?*" Sammi shouted, hiding behind Dink.

"Just my guinea pig," Dink said. "Loretta's real friendly. You want to hold her?"

"I am allergic to fur!" Sammi said, peering into the cage. "Don't let it out!"

"Okay, I won't," Dink said.

"Dink!" his mother called from downstairs. "Are you and Sammi ready for a snack?"

"Are you hungry?" Dink asked Sammi.

Sammi wrinkled his nose. "What are we having?"

Dink pretended to think, then said,

"Just the usual—rats' ears on crackers."

Sammi stared at Dink. "You are joking?"

"Yeah, I'm joking," Dink said. "Come on downstairs."

Dink's mother put a plate of peanut butter cookies and a quart of milk on the counter. Sammi inspected the cookies, then selected one.

"You're not allergic to cookies, are you?" Dink asked.

Sammi shook his head and took a small bite.

The doorbell rang, and Dink opened the door. Josh and Ruth Rose stood on the steps. Pal, Josh's basset hound, sat at their feet.

"We came to see if you and Sammi want to come out and play," Ruth Rose said. She held a purple Nerf football in her hand. The ball matched her purple jeans and sweatshirt.

"Hi, guys. Come on in," Dink said.

Josh made a beeline for the plate of cookies. Pal padded along behind him. His long pink tongue hung out of his mouth.

Sammi jumped onto a chair. "Keep it away!" he yelled. "I am allergic!"

Dink's mother put her hand on Sammi's shoulder. "It's okay, Sammi.

Josh, can Pal wait on the porch?"

"Sure, Mrs. D. Come on, boy," Josh said as he led Pal out of the room.

"Help yourselves, kids," Dink's mom said, pouring four glasses of milk.

Josh came back and grabbed two cookies. "Why're you wearing your bathrobe?" he asked Sammi.

"It is what we wear in my country," Sammi said, sipping his milk.

"I think it's beautiful," Ruth Rose said. "I wish I had one."

The doorbell rang again. This time it was Joan Klinker, Sammi's tutor. She had come in a taxi with Sammi's suitcases. Dink helped the driver carry them into the hallway.

"Hi, Sammi," she said. "How do you like this house?"

"There are animals here!" Sammi said. "I am allergic, you know."

"I'm afraid we have a guinea pig," Dink's mother said.

"Yes, and I saw the dog on the porch," Joan Klinker said. "I hope Sammi's allergies won't be too much trouble."

Dink's mother smiled. "I'm sure we'll make out fine," she said. "Dink, why don't you kids take Sammi's luggage up to his room before you go out to play?"

"May I come, too?" Joan Klinker asked. "I'd like to look at the room where Sammi will stay. Do you mind?"

"Not at all. Dink will show you the way."

Dink and Josh lugged the suitcases up the stairs, then plopped them down on Sammi's bed. Ruth Rose followed, with Sammi and his tutor right behind.

Joan Klinker walked around the room. She inspected the windows and tested the locks. She rattled the handles on the doors to the bathroom and hallway. "Do these doors have locks?" she asked Dink.

"Um, yeah, but we never use them," he answered.

"Is there a night-light?" she asked.

Dink pointed to a small blue light sticking from a wall socket.

Joan Klinker nodded. "I guess this will do," she said. "Now may I see Sammi's bathroom?"

Dink showed Joan the bathroom he and Sammi would share.

The woman checked out everything in the bathroom, then peeked into

Dink's room on the other side. "Who sleeps in here?" she asked.

"Me," Dink said. "My parents' room is downstairs."

"Do they have their own bathroom down there?" Joan asked.

Dink nodded as they walked back into Sammi's room.

Joan Klinker smiled at Dink. "This will be perfect!" she said. She patted Sammi on the head. "I'll see you later, okay?"

Sammi looked at her nervously. "Where are you going?"

"To my hotel room," Joan said. "But I'll come back after dinner for your French lesson." She took one more look around Sammi's room, then left.

"Do you play Nerf ball in your country?" Ruth Rose asked Sammi.

Sammi shook his head. "What is Nerf?"

"This," Josh said, tossing the foam ball to Sammi. It bounced off him and fell to the floor.

"Um, do you want to change?" Dink asked Sammi.

Sammi stared at his suitcase. "Your mother said she'd unpack for me," he said.

"She will," Dink said. "But for now, you can wear some of my stuff. Come on in my room."

The four kids trooped through the bathroom and into Dink's room. Loretta began running around her cage.

Dink found a pair of sweatpants and a sweatshirt in his closet. "These should fit," he told Sammi.

Sammi looked at the clothes but didn't take them from Dink.

"Who is going to dress me?" he asked.

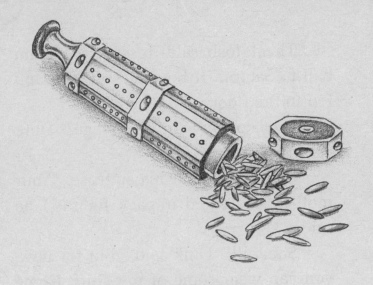

CHAPTER 3

Dink, Josh, and Ruth Rose stared at Sammi.

"Um, what do you mean, who's gonna dress you?" Dink asked.

"In my country, my servants dress me and undress me," Sammi said.

"Yeah, right," Josh said, grinning. "And my servants do my homework for me!"

"Do you really have servants?" Ruth Rose asked Sammi.

Sammi nodded. "I have five servants of my own. My father has twenty!"

"Twenty servants!" Josh yelled. "Are you guys rich?"

Sammi sat on Dink's bed. "We are very rich," he said. "My father is..."

Sammi didn't finish what he was going to say. Instead, he burst into tears.

"Great, Josh, you made him cry!" Dink said.

"I did not! I just asked him if he was rich!"

Ruth Rose sat next to Sammi. "Why are you crying?" she asked.

Sammi didn't answer. Big tears rolled down his cheeks.

Dink tossed the sweat clothes onto the bed. Then he ran into his bathroom and came out with a wad of tissues.

"Here," he said.

Sammi took the tissues and wiped his eyes.

"Do you miss your mom and dad?" Ruth Rose asked Sammi. "Is that why you're crying?"

Sammi took a deep breath and wiped at his tears. "I don't know where my parents are," he said. "They were kidnapped last week."

"KIDNAPPED!" the three other kids yelled.

Sammi nodded. "My father's ene-

mies snuck into the palace and took him and my mother."

"Palace?" Josh said. "You live in a palace? What are you, a prince or something?"

Sammi nodded. "Yes. My father is the king of Costra. I am Prince Samir Bin Oz. I will be king someday."

Sammi started crying again.

No one said anything. Even Loretta stopped running around in her cage.

Dink stared at Sammi. "You're a prince?" he finally asked. "Does my mom know all this, Sammi? I mean, about your folks being kidnapped and everything?"

The boy shook his head. "Only my tutor knows," he said. "My parents were kidnapped at night. I was sleeping. The next day I was snuck out of the palace and sent here so I would be safe."

"Safe from what?" Ruth Rose asked.

Sammi looked at her. His eyes were red and his nose dripped. "From the kidnappers," he said.

Just then, Pal started barking from the front porch.

"They're here!" Sammi cried. He jumped off the bed and ran into the bathroom.

Dink looked out the window. Pal was barking at a car. It was a taxi. Dink watched it turn the corner and disappear.

"Come on out, Sammi," Dink said. "It was just your tutor leaving."

Sammi stepped out of the bathroom. His eyes looked scared. "I am sorry," he whispered.

"No problem," Dink said. "Why don't we go down and play?"

He pointed to the sweat clothes on the bed. "Do you really need help getting dressed?"

Sammi took a deep breath and grinned. "No. I am in America now. I will learn to dress myself."

While Sammi changed, the other kids went outside and tossed the Nerf ball in Dink's backyard.

"It must be so cool to be a prince!" Josh said. "Just imagine ordering all those servants around!"

Dink bopped him with the Nerf ball.

"Josh, Sammi doesn't care about all that stuff," he said. "He misses his parents."

"I know," Josh said, "but still, just think. He could get ice cream in the middle of the night by snapping his fingers!"

Sammi came out dressed in Dink's sweat clothes.

Pal, tied to a tree, tried to lick Sammi's foot as he walked by.

Sammi jumped out of reach. "Is he trying to bite me?" he asked.

Josh laughed. "Naw, he's just saying hi," he said. "Pal wouldn't hurt a flea. Go ahead, pet him."

Sammi stepped closer and gave Pal a pat on his head. Then he sneezed.

"I like him," Sammi said. "But I am still allergic."

The kids taught Sammi the rules of touch football. They played until Dink's mother called them in to eat.

Promising to come over the next morning, Josh untied Pal and headed for home.

"Bye, Sammi!" Ruth Rose said. She cut through the hedge to her house next door.

"Your friends are nice," Sammi said. "Do you play together every day?"

"Sure," Dink said. "Don't you play with your friends in Co...in that place you come from?"

Sammi shook his head. "I have no friends. I stay in the palace and study with my tutors."

No friends? Dink stared at Sammi. He couldn't imagine not having Josh and Ruth Rose to hang out with.

"We better go wash up," Dink said, looking at his dirty hands. "I hope you like burgers and fries."

"Burgersandfries?" Sammi said. "What is burgersandfries?"

Dink grinned. "Hamburgers and French fries. French fries are skinny little potato slices. You dip them in ketchup."

Sammi let out a sigh. "Okay, I will try your food. Who will taste it for me?"

"Taste it?" Dink asked. "Why?"

"In my country," Sammi explained, "my father's enemies sometimes try to poison him. He has a servant taste our food to make sure it is safe."

Dink grinned at Sammi. "My mom's a real good cook. She doesn't use much poison at all!"

Sammi's eyes bugged out. "You are making a joke, right?"

"Yeah," Dink said. "But we have to tell her the truth about you, okay?"

"Why?" Sammi asked.

"Because it's the way we do things," Dink said. "Don't worry. You're safe here. Nobody will get you in Green Lawn."

CHAPTER 4

During supper, Dink and Sammi told Dink's mom the real reason why Sammi was in the United States.

"Oh, Sammi," Dink's mom said. "I am so sorry. Thank you for telling me."

After they all had some ice cream, Dink and his mother helped Sammi unpack. Dink's mother held up a long wooden box decorated with gold. "This is heavy, Sammi. What's inside?" she asked.

Sammi opened the lid and took out a shiny kaleidoscope. Its golden sides were encrusted with jewels.

"This kaleidoscope has been in my family for many years," Sammi explained. "It belonged to my grandfather's grandfather and *his* grandfather! Now it is my father's."

"What a lovely idea!" Dink's mother said. "Will the kaleidoscope belong to you someday?"

"On my fifteenth birthday, my father will give this to me," Sammi said. He frowned. "At least he would have, but now...I don't know what will happen."

Dink felt badly for Sammi. He couldn't imagine what he would feel like if his parents ever got kidnapped.

Dink's mother sat on the bed next to Sammi. She took his hand. "Sammi, I'm sure your parents will be found soon," she said. "Didn't you tell us that your father's friends are searching every corner of your country?"

Sammi nodded. "But his enemies are clever," he said. "They may have taken my parents far away from Costra."

Dink's mother gave Sammi a hug. Then she laid his pajamas and slippers on his bed. The pj's were red silk, and the slippers were purple velvet with floppy gold tassels.

"Pretty snazzy," Dink said, grinning at Sammi. "I usually sleep in an old T-shirt and shorts!"

Just then, the front doorbell rang. Dink's mother left the room.

"Watch," Sammi said, kneeling on the floor. He unscrewed the large end of the kaleidoscope and poured out all the pieces of glass. They made a red, yellow, and blue mound on the rug.

"It comes apart!" Dink said. He picked up some of the glass. The thin pieces felt smooth in his fingers.

A knock came at the door to Sammi's room. Joan Klinker poked her head in. "Hi, Sammi," she said.

Sammi smiled and scooped up the glass. "I'm showing Dink my kaleidoscope," he said. Dink helped Sammi put the kaleidoscope back in its box.

"Fine, Sammi," Joan said, looking at her watch. "It's almost eight. How about a short French lesson?"

She dropped a yellow book on Sammi's bed. "Will you excuse Sammi for a little while?" she said to Dink.

"Can't he stay?" Sammi asked. "Dink can have a lesson with me!"

Joan Klinker looked at Dink for a moment, then said, "Sure. Why not?"

"Great!" Dink said. He sat next to Sammi on the floor. Joan perched on the bed and opened the yellow book.

"First, some colors," Joan said. She pointed at Dink's shirt. "Blue. But in French, we say *bleu*. Repeat, Sammi."

Sammi said, *"Bleu."* To Dink, it sounded almost the same as "blue."

Joan pointed at Dink. "Now you, please."

"Bleu," said Dink, trying to imitate Sammi.

"Good!" Joan put a hand on Sammi's folded pajamas. "Red," she said.

"Rouge," said Sammi.

To Dink, it sounded almost like "rooj," so that's what he said.

Joan Klinker held up the yellow book. *"Jaune,"* she said. *"Le livre est jaune.* The book is yellow."

She pointed at Dink. "Can you say *jaune?"*

Dink blushed. "Joan," he finally said.

"No, Joan is my name," the tutor said.

Dink tried again. "Zhone," he said.

Sammi laughed. "That's okay," he said. "It took me a month to learn to say *jaune."*

"Now we will do some numbers," Joan said.

A half hour later, she closed the yellow book. "That's all for tonight," she said. "Tomorrow we will continue."

She checked the locks on Sammi's

window, his bathroom door, and the door out into the hall. Then she turned and smiled. *"Bonsoir,* Sammi."

"Bonsoir, madame," Sammi answered.

After Joan left, Dink stood up and yawned. "Night, Sammi. I'll wake you up for breakfast."

Dink headed into the bathroom and brushed his teeth. He smiled at his reflection in the mirror. Tomorrow, he decided, he'd learn how to say "My toothbrush is purple." In French!

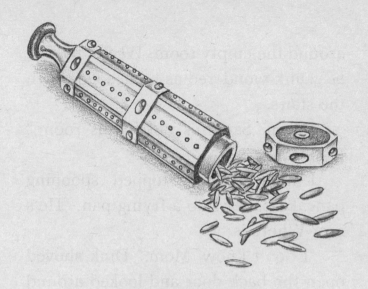

CHAPTER 5

The next morning, Dink washed his hands and face, then tapped on Sammi's bedroom door.

"Rise and shine!" Dink said. "We're having pancakes and sausages for breakfast!"

There was no answer. Dink opened the door and peeked in. Sammi's bed was mussed, but he wasn't in it.

"Sammi?" Dink said, glancing

around the empty room. *Where could he be?* Dink wondered as he headed down the stairs.

"Mom, Sammi's not in his room," Dink said.

Dink's mother stopped spooning pancake batter into a frying pan. "He's not? Where is he?"

"I don't know, Mom." Dink shoved open the back door and looked around the yard. "Not out here either," he said.

As Dink pulled the door shut again, his hand struck something sharp.

"Mom, look at this!" he yelled.

The wood around the door lock was shattered. Jagged slivers of wood stuck out. A few wood splinters lay on the floor under Dink's feet.

"Oh, my goodness!" his mother said. "Someone forced the door open!"

She turned and hurried up the hall stairs. Dink followed his mom into the guest room.

"Sammi?" his mom called. "Sammi, please answer! If you're hiding, please come out."

But Sammi did not answer.

"I'm calling Officer Fallon," Dink's mother said. "And Joan Klinker! Why don't you run next door and find out if Ruth Rose's family saw anything?"

Dink charged down the stairs and

out of the house. He tore into Ruth Rose's yard and banged his fist on her door.

Ruth Rose opened it, munching on a piece of toast.

"Have you seen Sammi?" Dink asked, out of breath.

She shook her head. "Why, is he missing?"

"Yes!" Dink said. "Someone broke in...Sammi's gone!"

"WHAT?" Ruth Rose yelled. "You mean he was kidnapped?"

Suddenly, Dink heard a siren. He left Ruth Rose with the toast in her hand and raced back to his front yard.

A police cruiser roared around the corner and whipped into his driveway. As the siren died, Officers Fallon and Keene burst out of the car.

Dink's mom came flying out of the house. Her face was white. "Thank

goodness you came," she told the officers. "I think our house guest has been
kidnapped!"

Just then, a yellow taxi pulled up in
front of Dink's house. The rear door
flew open, and Joan Klinker climbed
out.

"What has happened to Sammi?"
she called, running across the front
yard.

"We don't know," Dink's mother
said. "He's not in the house, and the
lock on our back door has been forced
open."

Joan Klinker put her hand to her
mouth. She swayed, then started to top-
ple. Officer Keene caught her just
before she fell.

"Bring her inside," Dink's mother
said, running for the front door.

"Take a look around," Officer Fallon
told Officer Keene. Then he helped

Dink's mother take Joan Klinker into the house.

Ruth Rose appeared through the hedge that separated their yards. She was dressed in blue bib overalls, a blue shirt, and blue high-top sneakers.

"Is Sammi really gone?" she asked Dink. "This isn't a joke, is it?"

Dink shook his head. His mouth was so dry he could hardly swallow. "I think it's real," he said, remembering what Sammi had told them about his father's enemies.

"But how could anyone just walk in and take him?" Ruth Rose asked.

"Our back door lock is busted," Dink said. "They must have gotten in that way."

Ruth Rose's mom and dad joined them as Dink explained.

"Let's all search the street," Ruth Rose's dad suggested. He went to organize the neighbors.

Just then, Josh arrived with his dog. "What's going on, Dinkus?" he asked. "Why's the cruiser here?"

"Sammi is gone," Dink said. "We think he's been kidnapped!"

Josh's mouth dropped open. Then he grinned. "This is a joke, right?"

Dink shook his head. "Come on, I'll show you where the kidnappers broke the kitchen door."

Dink started for the front steps. But before he reached the door, it opened. Joan Klinker and Dink's mother stepped out.

"Are you sure you're all right, Joan?" Dink's mother asked. "Won't you stay for a while?"

Joan Klinker shook her head. "I have to make some phone calls," she muttered. Then she hurried into the cab and it pulled away.

"That poor woman," Dink's mom said, heading back to the kitchen.

As Dink climbed the porch steps, something shiny caught his eye.

He bent down and picked up a small piece of yellow glass.

"What's that?" Ruth Rose asked.

Dink stared at the yellow sliver. He remembered where he'd seen others just like it.

"This came out of Sammi's kaleidoscope!" he said.

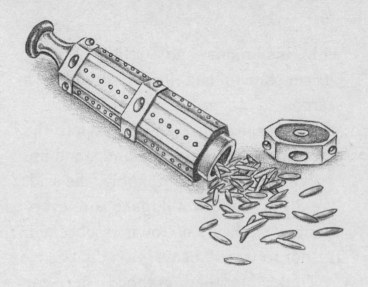

CHAPTER 6

Inside the house, Officer Fallon examined the piece of glass. "If this came out of the boy's kaleidoscope, how'd it get to your front steps?" he asked.

"The top unscrews," Dink explained. "Sammi likes to take the glass out."

Josh and Ruth Rose stood silently in Dink's kitchen. Pal lay at Josh's feet, snoozing. Dink was sitting at the table with his mom and Officer Fallon. Officer Keene had left to organize a search.

Officer Fallon sighed. He left the piece of glass on the table and stood up.

"Green Lawn isn't that big," he said. "We'll find the boy. I'll make sure every possible way out of town is checked. Try not to worry, okay?"

Dink's mother grabbed her car keys. "I'm going to drive around and look for him," she said.

"Can we come, too?" Dink asked.

His mother shook her head. "You can help by staying by the phone," she said. She looked at Officer Fallon. "Do you think the kidnappers would telephone here?"

Officer Fallon nodded. "They might try to make contact. But kidnappers usually wait a few days before calling. They like to get the family worried so they'll hand over more ransom money."

Dink watched his mother and Officer Fallon leave. He heard the front door lock click into position.

"Look at this," Dink said. He showed Josh and Ruth Rose the damaged back door.

"Boy, this is creepy!" Josh said.

"Poor Sammi," Ruth Rose said. "He must be so scared!"

"Let's go check out his room," Dink said. "Maybe we'll find some more clues."

The kids hurried toward the stairs. Pal followed them into Sammi's room, his long ears brushing the floor.

Sammi's sheet and blanket were tangled, half off the bed. Dink walked over to the bureau. There was the kaleidoscope box and two small mounds of colored glass. Each mound was a different color.

"This is the kaleidoscope," Dink said, removing it from the box. "See, he took all the glass out."

Josh touched the jewels that decorated the kaleidoscope. "Are these real?" he asked.

"Sammi said they were," Dink answered.

Ruth Rose was examining the pieces of glass. "Where are the yellow pieces?" she asked.

"What do you mean?" Dink asked.

"The piece we found is yellow," she said. "But all I see here is red and blue. No yellow."

"That's weird," Dink said. "Let's look around."

The kids began to search Sammi's room for the yellow glass. Pal waddled around, sniffing everything.

Dink checked in the bathroom while Josh went through the clothes in the closet. Ruth Rose got down on her hands and knees and looked under the bed.

"Well, if there's yellow glass in this room, I don't know where it is," Josh said. He stepped away from the closet.

"WATCH OUT!" Ruth Rose yelled, stopping Josh in his tracks.

She snatched something from the carpet where Josh was about to step. It was another piece of yellow glass.

Just then, the phone rang.

Dink ran down the stairs and grabbed the phone on its third ring.

"Hello?"

Dink listened for a minute, then yelled up the stairs, "Hey, guys, it's Officer Fallon. He wants to know if Sammi's pajamas and slippers are in his room. Can you look?"

He waited. Ruth Rose came to the top of the stairs. "No pj's or slippers," she said.

Dink spoke into the phone. "We can't find them."

After a minute, Dink hung up the phone. He climbed the stairs to Sammi's room.

"What's up with the slippers?" Josh asked.

"Ron Pinkowski found a gold tassel near the river by his bait shop," Dink said. "Sammi's slippers had gold tassels on them."

"But what—"

"And one of Mr. Pinkowski's boats is missing," Dink interrupted.

He stared at his two friends. "Officer Fallon thinks the kidnappers took Sammi away in a boat!"

CHAPTER 7

"What kind of boat?" Josh asked. "The water in Indian River isn't very deep."

"But it's deep enough for a row-boat," Ruth Rose said.

Dink thought about the river near Ron's Bait Shop. They'd all waded there before. The water was only up to their knees.

"Yeah," he said. "Maybe they took Sammi downriver in a small boat.

When they got to the deep part, they could have put him in a bigger boat..."

"...and taken him out to sea!" Ruth Rose added.

The kids stared at each other. Dink thought about poor Sammi, afraid of noises and animals, tied up in some boat.

"We have to do something, guys," he said. "Let's go see if we can find more clues at the bait shop." He ran down the stairs to the kitchen.

Ruth Rose hurried after him, with Josh and Pal right behind her.

"Your mom told us to stay put," Josh reminded Dink.

"I know, Josh." Dink was scribbling on a pad. "I'm telling her where we're going," he said. "We'll probably be back before she sees this. Come on!"

The kids cut through the dining room and headed for the back door.

Suddenly, Pal barked and began straining on his leash. He pulled until Josh let him have his way. Pal headed for the living room, and the kids followed.

"I think he smells something," Josh said. Pal had his nose on the rug, sniffing at something small and shiny.

"It's another piece of glass!" Josh said, snatching it away from the dog's nose.

"This is the third one," Dink said. He looked at the stairs going up to the bedrooms. "Sammi dropped one in his room, one down here, and another one on the front steps..."

"SAMMI LEFT US A TRAIL!" Ruth Rose suddenly yelled.

"I'll bet you're right," Dink said. "The kidnappers must have brought him down the stairs and out the front door. Come on, let's look for more!"

The kids hurried out the door and

into the front yard. Pal snuffled with his nose along the ground while the kids searched with their eyes.

"Nothing," Dink muttered after a few minutes. "The trail ends here."

Suddenly, Pal yanked on the leash.

"Whoa, doggie," Josh said.

But Pal kept pulling. He dragged Josh to the road. At the curb, Pal's nose went right into the gutter.

"Look!" Josh said. He held up a fourth piece of yellow glass.

Dink and Ruth Rose ran over. "Sammi must've dropped it when the kidnappers loaded him into a car," Ruth Rose said.

"And I bet the trail picks up again down at the river," Dink said. "Let's go!"

With Pal loping along behind them, the kids hurried down Woody Street. They cut past the elementary school, then crossed Duck Walk Way toward the river.

Inside his shop, Ron Pinkowski was feeding the bait shiners in one of his huge tanks.

"Hey, I heard about that boy disappearing," Ron said when he saw the kids.

"He didn't disappear," Josh said. "He was kidnapped!"

Ron nodded. "That's what Officer Fallon said. And they stole one of my rowboats!"

"Can you show us where the boat was?" Dink asked.

"Sure, come on." Ron took the kids outside. "Right over there," he said, pointing to a line of upside-down boats along the riverbank. There was an empty space between two of the boats.

"They broke my padlock and took a pair of my brand-new oars, too."

"Thanks, Mr. P," Dink said.

The kids hurried over to the row of boats and searched for yellow glass. Pal sniffed the ground for a few seconds, then flopped under a tree and closed his eyes.

The kids examined the ground where the boat had been. They didn't find any glass at all. "Let's look in the driveway," Dink suggested.

They walked back to the road, then

worked their way down to the boats
again.

Josh found a nickel, but there
wasn't a piece of yellow kaleidoscope
glass anywhere.

"That's weird," said Dink. "If
Sammi left a trail back at my house,
why didn't he drop another piece of
glass when he got here?"

"Maybe he ran out of glass," Josh
said.

Ruth Rose shook her head. "How could he? He took all the yellow glass, remember?"

"You know," Dink said, "something about the yellow glass is bugging me. Why did Sammi leave a yellow trail? Why not red or blue?"

"Well, he had the colors in separate little piles," Josh said. "So maybe he just grabbed the closest pile and it was yellow."

Ron Pinkowski walked over. "What're you kids looking for?" he asked.

Dink explained about the trail of yellow glass. "You didn't see any, did you?"

"Nope. Just that tassel thing, and I gave it to Officer Fallon."

"Did you hear a car last night?" Ruth Rose asked.

Ron grinned. "The way I snore? A

tank could drive down here and I'd snooze right through it!"

"Let's go back and see if my mom is home," Dink said. "She might have found out something. Thanks, Mr. P."

The kids and Pal hurried back to Dink's house. His mom was on the phone, looking worried. She made a motion for the kids to sit.

They did, with Pal at their feet. A minute later, Dink's mother hung up the phone.

"That was Officer Fallon," she said. "The police are searching everywhere. They're checking the train station, the airport, and every boat on the river, but so far, they aren't having any luck."

Dink's mother looked at the kids with concern in her eyes.

"How could a boy just disappear without a trace?" she asked.

CHAPTER 8

"Sammi left a trail, Mom," Dink said.

"He what?"

Dink explained about the pieces of yellow glass.

"Oh, my goodness!" Dink's mother grabbed the phone, dialed quickly, and handed the phone to Dink. "Tell Officer Fallon," she said.

Dink talked and Officer Fallon listened. "But when we got to Ron's Bait

Shop, we didn't find any more glass," Dink said into the phone.

He nodded, said, "Uh-huh," then hung up.

"Officer Fallon wants all the glass we found," Dink said. He pulled the four little pieces out of his pocket.

His mother picked up the phone. "I think I'll go visit Joan Klinker," she said. "She must be frantic, and she's all alone there at the hotel."

She dialed another number. "Hello, Joan? This is Dink's mom, Mrs. Duncan," she said into the phone. "Would you like some company? May I come over?"

Dink couldn't hear Joan's answer, but his mother smiled. "Okay, fine. I'll be there in five minutes," she said before hanging up.

She glanced into the mirror, then headed for the door. "We're meeting for coffee at Ellie's," she said. "Oh, let me have the pieces of glass. I can take them to the police station after I meet Joan."

Dink dropped the yellow glass into his mother's hand. She smiled weakly at the kids, then hurried out the back door.

Dink stared at the door, thinking.

"Earth to Dink," Josh said, snapping his fingers in front of Dink's nose.

Dink shook his head. "Something my mother said made me think of something else, but now I forgot!"

"You forgot what your mother said, or you forgot what it made you think of?" Ruth Rose asked.

"Both!" Dink said, giving Josh a look. "I was just getting it when you snapped your fingers!"

"Sorry," Josh said. "Why don't we have a snack? Maybe your memory needs some ice cream."

Ruth Rose laughed. "Better feed him, Dink. You know how he gets when his tummy is empty."

Dink sighed. "We finished the ice cream last night," he said, heading for the kitchen. He pulled open the refrigerator. "But we've got Cool Whip and cherry Jell-O."

He grabbed the bowl and handed it to Josh. "Here, are you..."

Then Dink stopped. He stared at the bowl of Jell-O. "That's it!" he yelled. "It's yellow!"

Josh shook his head. "Dinkus, this is red Jell-O, not yellow Jell-O."

"No—I mean, yes, I know. But Jell-O made me think of yellow!" Dink said.

"Can I eat while you talk?" Josh asked.

Dink got bowls and spoons and put them on the table. Then he continued. "After you guys left yesterday, Sammi's tutor came over and gave me and Sammi a French lesson," he said.

Josh grinned. "Say something in French," he said.

"Just eat, Josh, and let me finish!"

"Sorry," Josh said, plopping a gob of Cool Whip onto his Jell-O. He let Pal lick his spoon.

"Remember a few minutes ago when my mom said she was going to see Sammi's tutor?" Dink asked. "She called her Joan, remember?"

Josh and Ruth Rose nodded.

"That made me think of the French lesson yesterday. She taught me to say *yellow* in French. The word for *yellow* is *jaune*, only I pronounced it 'Joan,' like her name."

"Um, Dinkus?" Josh said. "What's this got to do with anything?"

"Don't you guys see?" Dink said. "The French word for *yellow* sounds just like 'Joan.' That's Sammi's tutor's name. Sammi could have left a trail of red or blue, but he chose the yellow glass. I think Sammi was trying to say 'Joan'!"

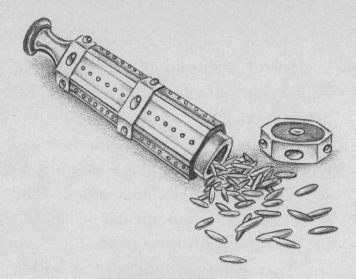

CHAPTER 9

"Maybe Sammi thinks Joan knows who the kidnappers are," Ruth Rose said.

"Maybe," Dink said. "Or maybe *Joan* is the kidnapper!"

Josh and Ruth Rose looked up from their Jell-O.

Josh had Cool Whip on his nose. "His tutor?" he asked.

"Think about it," Dink went on. "Sammi wakes up in the middle of the night. Someone's in his room. He recognizes Joan and grabs a pile of glass. Yellow glass, because he remembers how much her name sounds like the French word for *yellow*. And he knows I know that!"

"But how could she be the kidnapper?" Ruth Rose asked. "She's Sammi's friend. She came here to help him."

"Yeah, and you saw how upset she was this morning," Josh said. "That couldn't be an act. I still think Sammi just grabbed the first pile of glass his hand landed on in the dark."

Ruth Rose stood up. "There's one way to find out," she said. "Let's go to the hotel and talk to her."

"Okay," Dink said. "But she's not at the hotel. My mom said she was meeting Joan at the diner."

"Good!" Josh said, gulping down the last of his Jell-O. "I can get an ice cream while we talk!"

The kids took Pal and hurried to Ellie's Diner on Main Street. Dink glanced through the window, but he didn't see Joan Klinker or his mom.

"I wonder where they are. Mom's car isn't here either," Dink said, looking up and down Main Street.

"Let's ask Ellie," Ruth Rose suggested.

Josh pushed the door open and the kids stepped inside. Two teenagers were eating scrambled eggs, but no one else sat in the booths or at the counter.

"Hey there, kids," Ellie said. "Hi, cute poochie!" She bent down and patted Pal, then stroked his ears. "Shall I scoop up three cones?" she asked.

Dink shook his head. "No, thanks, I'm looking for my mom," he said. "Have you seen her? She was supposed to meet someone here a little while ago."

Ellie shook her head. "Nope, haven't seen your mother in a few days," she said.

"Maybe they're at the hotel," Ruth Rose said.

Dink nodded. "I guess it's worth a try," he said.

They thanked Ellie and headed for the Shangri-la Hotel, two blocks up Main Street.

"Why couldn't we at least get cones to go?" Josh asked. He placed one hand dramatically across his forehead. "I think I feel faint."

"Later," Dink said. "After we find Sammi." *And after we find my mom,* he thought.

Three minutes later, they walked into the hotel. Mr. Linkletter was sitting on one of the lobby chairs, eating a doughnut and sipping coffee.

"Well, hello there," he said when the

trio approached him. He glanced at Pal. "Joshua, I assume your dog is, um, house-trained?"

Josh grinned as Pal flopped down at Mr. Linkletter's feet. "Yep, and he's hotel-trained, too!"

Mr. Linkletter twitched an eyebrow. "Well, then," he said, "how can I be of service today?"

"I'm looking for my mom," Dink said. "She was supposed to meet Joan Klinker at Ellie's, but they're not there. Have you seen them?"

Mr. Linkletter set his coffee down. "I didn't see your mom, but Ms. Klinker left the hotel a short while ago."

"Did she say where she was going?"

Mr. Linkletter shook his head. "Not a word."

Dink glanced around the hotel lobby. Where could his mother be? She always let him know if she had to change her plans. Always!

"She didn't leave a note or anything?"

"I'm sorry, Donald," Mr. Linkletter said. "Perhaps she's gone back home. Would you like to call her?"

Suddenly, Dink felt sick. He blinked back tears. Something was wrong! First Sammi disappeared, and now his mother was gone! And she'd been on her way to see Joan Klinker with the yellow glass!

Mr. Linkletter wiped his fingers on his napkin and stood up. "Come, you can use my phone," he said. He took Dink over to the counter. Pal followed Mr. Linkletter, sniffing at his heels.

Dink dialed and listened for his mother's voice on the other end. But no one answered.

He set the phone down and looked up at Mr. Linkletter. "Where could she be?" he asked.

CHAPTER 10

Just then, Pal began growling and biting at Mr. Linkletter's left shoe.

"What on earth?" Mr. Linkletter said, pulling his foot away.

But Pal wouldn't give up. Using his paws and teeth, he tried to pull Mr. Linkletter's shiny black loafer right off his foot.

"Joshua!" Mr. Linkletter said. "Please teach your dog some manners!"

"Take it off!" Ruth Rose suddenly said.

Mr. Linkletter glanced down at Ruth Rose. "I beg your pardon?"

"I think I know what Pal wants," she said. "Please take off your shoe!"

Mr. Linkletter let out a big sigh. "Very well. If that will bring peace!"

The tall man leaned over and removed his left shoe. He showed it to

Pal. "There, satisfied?" he asked.

Pal grabbed the shoe in his mouth and dropped it at Josh's feet.

"I WAS RIGHT!" Ruth Rose yelled. She picked up the shoe and held it upside down.

On the sole, stuck to a wad of gum, was a piece of shiny yellow glass.

"The dog was after a nasty piece of gum?" Mr. Linkletter asked.

"No," Dink said. "That piece of glass is from Sammi's kaleidoscope! This means the kidnappers brought Sammi here, to the hotel!"

"Donald, you're giving me a headache," Mr. Linkletter said, taking his shoe back. He pulled the gum off and slipped the loafer back on his foot. "Who is Sammi? *What* kidnappers?"

Dink told Mr. Linkletter about Sammi's disappearing from his bed. Then he explained about Joan Klinker's

French lesson, Sammi's kaleidoscope, and the trail of yellow glass.

"Now my mom's missing, too," Dink said. "And I think Joan Klinker kidnapped them both! She might be keeping them up in her room!"

"Um, Dink?" Josh said. "Officer Fallon said Sammi was taken away in a boat. How could he be in the hotel and in a boat at the same time?"

"I don't know," Dink said. "But I still want to check out Joan Klinker's room. That piece of glass on your shoe proves Sammi was here!"

Mr. Linkletter sighed and set down his half-eaten doughnut. "Very well," he said. "Ms. Klinker has room 301. I'll take you up there, but you must be very quiet. Our guests don't expect crowds of children parading about the halls." He looked down at Pal. "But the hound has to stay down here. The Shangri-la does *not* permit animals upstairs!"

"But he can smell stuff," Josh said. "We need him!"

Mr. Linkletter looked at Pal's big brown eyes. "Oh, all right. What's one more broken rule?"

The kids and Pal followed Mr. Linkletter into the elevator.

When it stopped on the third floor, they all walked quickly to room 301. A man in a white uniform was pushing a cart full of linens down the hall and around the corner.

Mr. Linkletter unlocked the door and pushed it open.

Joan Klinker's bed was made and two suitcases stood on the floor.

"Do your thing," Josh whispered into Pal's ear.

Pal walked in a wide circle, sniffing the carpet. Suddenly, he made a beeline for the closet and began scratching at the door.

Josh opened the closet door and Pal rushed in.

Dink noticed that the closet was empty. Joan Klinker had packed everything.

"What's in there, boy?" Josh asked, getting down on his hands and knees.

While Pal and Josh searched the closet floor, Dink and Ruth Rose looked under the bed and in the bathroom.

Suddenly, Josh backed out of the closet. "Look what Pal found!" he cried. In his hand, he held a small piece of yellow glass.

"You were right, Dink," Ruth Rose said. "Sammi must have been in this room!"

Just then, Pal raced from the room with his nose to the floor. The next thing they heard was Pal barking and growling.

Everyone followed him, just in time to see Pal attack the white linen cart.

He bit at the side of the cart and tried to pull it back along the floor.

The man in the white uniform pushed the cart in the other direction.

"Get outta here, mutt!" the man yelled, kicking at the dog.

That wasn't a good idea. Pal grabbed the man's pants cuff in his teeth and began thrashing and growling.

"Pal, no!" Josh shouted. He pulled Pal away, but the hound was still barking at the man.

Mr. Linkletter looked at the man. "Who are you?" he asked.

"Just collectin' the laundry," the man said, glaring at Pal.

Mr. Linkletter pointed to the words stitched into the man's shirt. "But we don't use Ace Laundry Service," he said.

Suddenly, the man bolted for the

elevator. But he tripped over Pal's leash and fell on his face.

Mr. Linkletter moved spryly and sat on the man's back. "What are you doing in this building?" he demanded.

"I ain't talkin'!" the man mumbled with his face in the carpet.

"Help me, guys," Dink said, grabbing the side of the cart. With a solid yank, the kids toppled it over.

A mountain of sheets and towels piled out onto the floor.

In the bottom of the cart lay Sammi, tied and gagged.

CHAPTER 11

The three kids slid Sammi out of the cart and laid him gently on the floor. While Dink and Josh worked on the knots, Ruth Rose pulled away his gag.

Before Sammi could speak, Pal waddled over and covered his face with wet dog kisses.

Sammi gave Pal a big hug. Then he sneezed.

They all jumped when the elevator door slid open and Joan Klinker stepped

out. When she saw Sammi and the man on the floor, her face turned as white as the sheets.

"You—you've found Sammi!" Joan said, rushing to his side.

"Ain't that cute!" the man on the floor said. "Well, I ain't taking this rap alone! She's the one planned the whole thing! We done it together."

"What are you talking about?" Joan said. "I—I've never seen this man in my life!"

The man let out a cackle. "What a

lousy thing to say about your own husband!" he said.

Just then, the elevator door slid open again. Dink's mother and Officer Fallon stepped into the hallway.

"Well, well," Officer Fallon said. "Good thing I brought two pairs of handcuffs!"

An hour later, Joan Klinker and her husband, Nick, were in jail.

Mr. Linkletter went back to finish eating his doughnut.

Dink, Josh and Pal, Ruth Rose, Sammi, and Dink's mom joined Officer Fallon in the police station.

"You were pretty clever to leave that trail of yellow glass," Officer Fallon told Sammi.

"Thank you," Sammi said. "I hoped Dink would remember that the French word for yellow sounds like 'Joan.'"

"I did remember," Dink said. "But Josh's dog was the one who found most of the glass."

Josh beamed and patted Pal's head. "Good dog," he said.

"Well, Ms. Klinker and her husband sang like little birds," Officer Fallon said. "They planned this thing carefully. After they stashed Sammi in the closet upstairs, they brought one of his slipper tassels to the river to throw us off the trail."

"I heard them talking in the car," Sammi said. "They were going to take me back to Costra. I would have disappeared, just like my parents. Then my father's enemies would have taken over our country."

Dink looked at his mom. "How did you know we were at the hotel?" he asked.

"Well, I met Joan outside Ellie's,"

Dink's mother said. "She said she was happy to be out of the hotel and suggested we go for a walk. Naturally, we talked about the kidnapping, and she mentioned Sammi's slipper tassel being found at the river."

"Which she shouldn't have known about, right?" said Ruth Rose.

Dink's mother smiled. "Right. And when I happened to mention the trail of yellow glass, she suddenly hurried away. She said she had something important to do at the hotel. So I came right here to see Officer Fallon."

Officer Fallon smiled at the three kids. "But by the time we got to the hotel, you three had everything under control."

Just then, Officer Fallon's computer said, "You've got mail!"

"Ah, I've been waiting for this e-mail," he said.

He moved his computer mouse,

clicked twice, and smiled. "You should all hear this, so I'll read it aloud.

"The king and queen of Costra have been found, thanks to your tip. They are alive and well. Both send love to their son. Want him to come home immediately."

Everyone in the office cheered. Sammi looked shocked, and then he beamed.

"But how did you find them?" he asked Officer Fallon.

"Your kidnappers spilled the beans," he said. "They were hired by the same guys who kidnapped your parents. They gave me names and places, so I just e-mailed the Costran police."

The next day, Dink, Josh, Pal, and Ruth Rose said good-bye to Sammi. Each of the kids gave him a wrapped gift. Pal's gift for Sammi was a big, wet lick on the cheek.

Sammi smiled, then sneezed.

Three weeks later, a large package arrived at Dink's house. It was from Costra and addressed to all three kids.

"Dibs on the cool stamps!" Josh said.

Dink opened the parcel and found four smaller packages labeled DINK, JOSH, RUTH ROSE, and PAL.

Dink and Josh found small gold kaleidoscopes in their packages. Their names were spelled on the sides with tiny rubies.

"What'd he send you?" Josh asked Ruth Rose.

"OH, MY GOSH!" she screamed and held up a dark blue robe just like Sammi's.

"Here's a picture and a note," Dink said. He read the note aloud.

The picture showed Sammi wearing the gifts the kids had given him—Ruth Rose's sweatshirt, Josh's jeans, and Dink's baseball cap.

Dear friends,
I miss you. My father says you can come here and visit someday. You can even bring Pal!
Your friend,
Sammi Bin Oz

Suddenly, Pal let out a woof. "He wants us to open his package," Josh said.

He helped Pal rip off the paper. Inside, they found a purple velvet doggy sweater. GOOD DOG had been stitched into the velvet with gold thread.

Dear Readers,

I hope you enjoyed reading *The Kidnapped King.* In this book, Dink, Josh, and Ruth Rose have a new friend. He is a basset hound, and you

Dorian Ponds

first met him in *The Invisible Island.* I didn't know what to name Josh's new dog, so I asked for your help. Boy, did you come through for me! I received plenty of great ideas. It was a hard decision, but I finally chose Pal for the dog's new name. Pal will be a pal for Josh and his friends. Thanks to all of you who sent in names.

Dorian Ponds suggested Pal as the dog's name. Dorian attends Belleair School in Clearwater, Florida. Thank you, Dorian! I'm sure that Josh thinks Pal is a fine name for his pooch.

Please visit my Web site at
www.ronroy.com or send your letters to:

Ron Roy
c/o Random House Children's Books
1745 Broadway, Mail Drop 11-2
New York, NY 10019

Happy reading!

Sincerely,

Ron Roy

Collect clues with Dink, Josh, and Ruth Rose in their next exciting adventure,

THE LUCKY LOTTERY

Dink looked around the room. "What did the burglars take?" he asked.

"Lottery tickets," Lucky said. "My grandfather always sends us lottery tickets for Christmas. This morning, he called. He told me that my ticket was the big winner! I ran in here to get it, but it was gone."

"Um, how much was the lottery ticket worth?" Dink asked.

Lucky dropped into a chair. "Seven big ones," he said.

"Seven thousand dollars?" Josh squeaked.

"No," Lucky said, shaking his head. "Seven *million.*"